Where is S

by Michèle Dufresne

Illustrated by Cula Carmen Elena

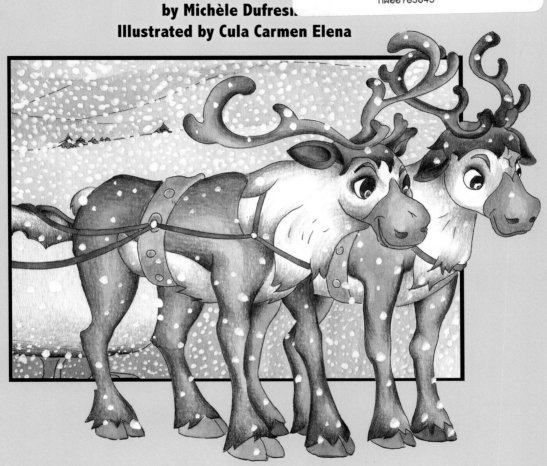

Pioneer Valley Educational Press, Inc.

"Little Elf, where is Santa?"
said Mrs. Claus.
"The sleigh is ready to go.
The reindeer are ready to go."

3

Little Elf looked and looked for Santa.
"Santa! Santa! Where are you?"
shouted Little Elf.

Little Elf went into Santa's workshop.
"I can see the toys.
I can see the dolls,
and I can see the cars.
But where is Santa?"

Little Elf went outside.
He went to look on Santa's sleigh.
"I can see the presents,
and I can see the reindeer.
But where is Santa?"

Little Elf and Mrs. Claus
looked for Santa.
They looked and looked.
"Santa! Santa! Where are you?"
they shouted.

"Ho! Ho! Ho!" said Santa.

"Look!" said Mrs. Claus.
"Here is Santa.
He is in the kitchen eating cookies."

"Come on, Santa," said Little Elf.
"The sleigh is ready to go.
The reindeer are ready to go."

Santa patted his belly.
"Ho! Ho! Ho!" said Santa.
"And I'm ready to go, too!"